LEO'S LADDER

Written by Dee Griffiths

Illustrated by Ali Holah

2018

See what else Leo is up to—visit the author's website
www.deegriffiths.com
Visit Ali's website to discover more of her art
www.aliholah.com

Leo's Ladder

Imprint Digital, UK
Cataloging information
ISBN: 978-1-916502-90-1

Credits
Editor: Nicci Robinson @ Global Wordsmiths
Production Design: Nicci Robinson @ Global Wordsmiths

LEO'S LADDER

Written by Dee Griffiths

Illustrated by Ali Holah

One day Leo found a ladder outside his house. Leo was thrilled! He thought he could really use a ladder. He'd been hoping for a ladder and felt his wish had come true.

But his mum and dad thought it very surprising indeed.

"But who does it belong to?" asked his mum.

"It must be for me," Leo hoped.

His dad simply said, "Someone must have lost it. Let's see if we can find the owner."

So off they all went to find the ladder's owner.

Leo walked down the lane with his mum and dad telling them stories about what he would love to do with a ladder of his very own. It seemed to Leo that ladders were everywhere.

Leo asked at the fire station. But the brigade had all their ladders, and Leo's ladder wasn't long enough to reach the top of tall buildings.

"Look here, Leo," said the fearless fireman. "We keep our ladders on the engine."

Leo asked at the library. "Are you finding it hard to reach the books on the very top shelves?" he asked the librarian.

"Thank you for asking. But we have our library ladder right here," whispered the librarian.

The shopkeeper wasn't missing a ladder either. He had a brand new one and proudly showed it to Leo.
"But that is a fine ladder," he said. Shopkeepers know these things.

In the park, the gardener was standing on a ladder watering the hanging baskets. Leo smiled a secret smile. "I hope this ladder doesn't belong to anyone," Leo told his parents.

"Who else could possibly be missing a ladder?" asked his mum.
Leo said, "Please let's go back. We've tried very hard to find the ladder's home."
So Mum, Dad, and Leo headed home.

At bedtime, Leo couldn't sleep for excitement. Finally, a ladder of my own, he thought. "Finders, keepers!" Leo's heart sang.
He loved the ladder already! Leo couldn't stop thinking of all the fun they'd have together.

Lying in bed, in the darkness, Leo wondered who really owned the ladder. I bet they're really missing it, he thought.

He flicked on the light, grabbed some crayons and a piece of paper, and got to work. Leo now knew he had to find its owner.
He wanted a ladder, that's for certain, but there was someone else out there who was missing their ladder.

At breakfast, Leo leaned forward and announced, "I've been thinking. We need to try again today."
Leo proudly showed his poster to his mum and dad.

And so the family set off again to find the ladder's owner.
"This is turning into a real adventure!" exclaimed Leo.

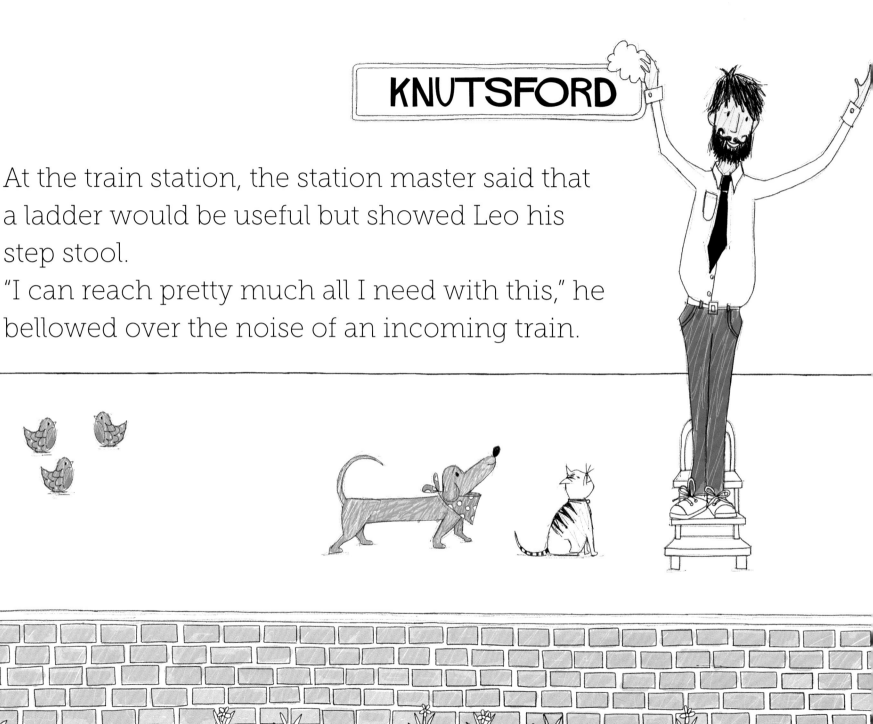

KNUTSFORD

At the train station, the station master said that a ladder would be useful but showed Leo his step stool.

"I can reach pretty much all I need with this," he bellowed over the noise of an incoming train.

And the street lighting team used huge cherry pickers on trucks to reach so high. "We used to use ladders, but now we've gone big. See?"

The window cleaner looked longingly at Leo's ladder. He always needed a good ladder, but he had a multi-purpose folding ladder to help him do his job.

Heading home, they saw a house
with a magnificent tree house.
Leo could see straight away that
this was the ladder's home.
"Stop! This is it!" shouted Leo.
"You're absolutely right, Son,"
replied Dad.

A small boy with curly hair stood on the grass below the tree house looking very sad.

"This must be yours," announced Leo to the gloomy-
looking boy.
"It is! Thank you so much," he replied happily. "I'm
George, and this is my tree house."
"It's wonderful. And I love your ladder." Leo grinned,
happy to have reunited it with its owner.
"Would you like to come up and play?" he asked.

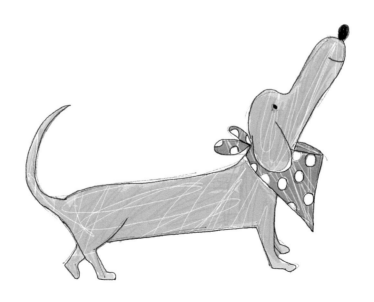

So Leo and George climbed up the ladder into the tree house. "Wow, this is a wonderful tree house," said Leo. "I can see why you really need this ladder."

"I thought my ladder was gone for good, and you brought it back to me," said George. "Now we can play up here whenever we like."

Leo smiled from ear to ear. The ladder really did make him happy.

But not as much as having a new friend.

Explore more of Leo's world:

Editing & production
Global Wordsmiths
& Global Words Press

www.deegriffiths.com
www.aliholah.com

www.globalwords.co.uk